You're Invited to Mary-Kate & Ashley's
HAWAIIAN BEACH PARTY™

by Nancy E. Krulik

DUALSTAR PUBLICATIONS PARACHUTE PRESS, INC.

SCHOLASTIC INC.
New York   Toronto   London   Auckland   Sydney

DUALSTAR PUBLICATIONS   PARACHUTE PRESS, INC.

Dualstar Publications   Parachute Press, Inc.
c/o 10100 Santa Monica Blvd.   156 Fifth Avenue
Suite 2200   Suite 325
Los Angeles, CA 90067   New York, NY 10010

Published by Scholastic Inc.

With special thanks to Robert Thorne, Harold Weitzberg, and Hilton Hawaiian Village.

Printed in the U.S.A.
April 1997
ISBN: 0-590-88012-8
A B C D E F G H I J

"It's Saturday! Hooray for the weekend!" I shouted.

I'm Mary-Kate Olsen. My sister, Ashley, and I are twins. We're both nine years old. We both have strawberry blond hair and big, blue eyes.

We look alike, but we don't always think alike.

I think weekends are for taking it easy. But Ashley doesn't agree.

"*I* think we should start our homework today," Ashley told me. "And I think we should do our weekend chores tomorrow."

Now *I* think we have a *big* problem!

"Sorry, Ashley," I said. "But I need a break. So let's do chores *after* we have a little fun!"

Hmmmm. Ashley looked thoughtful. "Okay. But what should we do?"

I grabbed the phone. "Let's call our friends and ask them!"

"Right!" Ashley said. "We can speak to them all at the same time on our special phone."

I called Nicole, Jenny, and Cheryl. "Listen, everybody," I told them. "We have a question!"

"What's the very *best* way to have fun?" Ashley asked.

"That's easy," Nicole said. "Playing catch is the most fun."

"No way! Going swimming is the best way to have fun," Jenny said.

"You're both wrong," Cheryl said. "The absolute best way to have fun is to play music and dance."

Jenny, Nicole, and Cheryl began to argue.

"Don't fight, you guys!" I said. "I know how we can do *all* those things!"

"We'll have a party!" I said. "But not just *any* party. We'll have a beach party!"

Everyone cheered.

"Great idea! We can ride our bikes to the beach around the corner," Nicole said.

"We *always* ride our bikes to *that* beach," Cheryl told her. "What's fun about that? Besides, I'm not sure a beach party is really the best idea."

"Sure, it is," Jenny said. "As long as we go to a special beach."

"I know where the beaches are *really* special," I said. "Hawaii!"

I pulled out a picture postcard that our family received in the mail. Hawaii looked amazing!

"Hawaii has fantastic beaches," Nicole agreed. "I know, because I lived there when I was little."

"But isn't it far out in the Atlantic Ocean?" Jenny asked.

"No, Hawaii is in the Pacific Ocean," Cheryl told her. "Everyone knows that."

Ashley and I rolled our eyes. Cheryl is always correcting us. Sometimes it gets annoying.

"Wherever it is, Hawaii sounds great," Jenny said. "But how will we get there?"

"Don't worry about that," I said. "Just pack up your bathing suits. Then meet Ashley and me at the marina, where everyone keeps their boats."

An hour later we met at the marina.

"I'm not so sure we should travel on the water," Cheryl said. She pushed a strand of blond hair behind her ear.

"Oh, we won't travel *on* the water," I told her. "We'll travel *under* the water. In that—a submarine!"

I pointed to the huge, sparkling white boat that was waiting for us. Jenny, Nicole, and Cheryl gasped.

"Wow! A submarine!" they all yelled at once.

We raced onto the submarine's main deck. "Next stop, Hawaii!" I called.

The submarine dove deep under the ocean and headed straight for Hawaii. We were there in no time at all.

The submarine slowly rose to the water's surface. It pulled up to a dock and stopped.

"This is fantastic!" I shouted. "I can't believe I'm really looking at—"

"*Why key-key,*" Cheryl said.

"Why *what?*" Ashley asked.

"*Why key-key* is how you say W-A-I-K-I-K-I," Cheryl said. "Waikiki is a famous beach. People come here from all over the world."

"They should," Ashley said. "Because Waikiki is beautiful!"

We raced down the long dock, heading toward dry land.

"Last one on the beach is a rotten coconut!" I called.

We ran onto the beach and set up our chairs. We put on sunglasses and sunblock.

"All set!" I cheered. "I can't believe we're really here."

"Then you need an official welcome. *A luau!*" Jenny called out.

"What's a *loo-ow?*" I asked.

"*A luau* means welcome in Hawaiian," Jenny said.

Cheryl frowned. "Actually a *luau* is a delicious Hawaiian feast.

"*Aloha* means welcome, or hello," Cheryl added. "It can also mean friendship and good-bye."

"Who cares what it means?" Jenny said. "I say hello to Hawaii. Because I never want to say good-bye to this amazing blue water!"

"I don't want to say hello *to* the water," Ashley told her. "I want to say hello *in* the water!"

She started to kick off her shoes. "I'm going for a swim!"

"No, Ashley! Don't!" Cheryl yelled.

"What's wrong?" Ashley asked. "Why can't I go in the water?"

"You're not wearing your bathing suit," Cheryl pointed out. "Besides, we didn't have anything to eat yet. And I'm starving!"

"I'm a little hungry, too," I said.

"So let's eat pineapples," Cheryl said. "They grow the best pineapples in Hawaii."

"I want to get right in the water," Nicole said.

"Yeah, me too," Jenny added.

"But *I* said *my* idea first," Cheryl replied.

Uh-oh.

Ashley and I exchanged worried looks. Our *beach* party was becoming an *arguing* party!

"Ashley! What should we do?" I whispered.

"Don't worry," Ashley told me. "I have an idea!"

Ashley put two fingers in her mouth and let out a whistle.

"Listen up, everybody!" she cried. "Nicole used to live in Hawaii. So we should let her choose what to do first."

Everyone but Cheryl agreed.

"Okay, then I guess it's *kai* time," Nicole said.

"What does *kai* mean?" I asked.

"*Kai* is the Hawaiian word for ocean," Nicole explained. "I say, let's hit the water!"

We quickly changed into our bathing suits. We were ready to swim.

"All right!" I shouted. "Last one in the *kai* is a rotten pineapple!"

We grabbed bright, colored rafts. It was time for some serious splashing and floating in the shallow water.

I noticed that Cheryl was the last one in. But soon she was splashing along with the rest of us.

"Now, this is *fun!*" Jenny squealed. "Let's head into the deeper water. I want to swim!"

"Wait!" Cheryl shouted. "I know how to have much *more* fun." She ran out of the water and onto the beach. "Follow me!" she called.

Cheryl scooped up an armful of beach balls.

"We can play catch with these beach balls!" she said.

"Great! But let's play catch *in* the water!" Nicole called back.

We each grabbed a beach ball and ran back into the water. Ashley pulled Cheryl along with her.

"Here, Cheryl! Catch!" I yelled. I tossed a beach ball to Cheryl.

Splash!

Cheryl dropped the ball. "Oops!" she said. She picked it up and tossed it to Jenny.

We all played catch for a while. Then Cheryl headed out of the water. "I don't want to play anymore," she said.

"Wait! Playing catch was your idea," Nicole said.

"I'd rather play on the beach," Cheryl told her.

"They're arguing again," I whispered to Ashley.

"We'd better think of something else to do—fast!" Ashley replied.

A big wave rushed up behind me.

"Hey, everybody! Let's ride the waves!" I said.

"No, let's go back to that nice big dock and look at the fish." Cheryl grinned. "Did you know that there are hundreds of different fish in Hawaii?"

"There are thousands, but we want to do more than watch the fish," Nicole told her. "We want to be in the water."

"Uh-oh! They're *never* going to stop fighting," I whispered to Ashley.

"No problem," Ashley said. "Hey, I know how we can ride the waves *and* see spectacular fish, too!"

Ashley pulled a clear mask over her face. "Hey everyone! Grab a snorkel!"

We pulled on swimming masks and snorkel tubes to breathe through.

"With this snorkel gear, we can swim all day!" I said.

I dove through the waves. Ashley, Nicole, and Jenny dove in beside me.

The water was bright and clear. Colored fish swam right past our noses.

Finally we all popped up again.

"Snorkeling is incredible!" I said. "But where's Cheryl?"

23

I spotted Cheryl standing on the beach. "Cheryl! Put on your mask and join us," I called.

"No way! You guys come back here," Cheryl said.

I frowned. "Cheryl's missing all the fun," I told Ashley.

"Maybe we should do something else," Ashley replied.

"Great idea!" I exclaimed. "Hey, Cheryl, how would you like to do like *that?*" I asked. I pointed to two guys riding Jet Ski watercraft.

Cheryl laughed out loud. "You're joking, right?" She smiled. "We can't possibly do *that!*"

Whoooosh!

The two guys sped past us.

"Now that's what I call excitement!" I said.

"But we can't ride a Jet Ski without a grown-up," Ashley pointed out.

"No problem," Nicole said. "Those guys are my old friends, Honolulu Harry and Big Kahuna Cal. They'll be glad to give us a ride!"

Harry and Cal helped us pull on our life jackets. Then off we went!

We flew over the waves.

When we landed back onshore, Cheryl was still standing there.

"What happened to you?" I asked. "Don't you like to ride a Jet Ski, either?"

"No, I think it's boring," Cheryl said. "I'd rather do something really exciting."

"Cowabunga, dude!" Ashley exclaimed. "Let's surf! We could goofy-foot it through the clamshell!"

Ashley and I grabbed surfboards and planted them in the sand.

"You're in luck!" I told Cheryl. "The wet ones are fully pumping mondo corduroy to the horizon!"

Cheryl stared at us. "What are you two talking about?"

"Surfing!" Ashley said. "I said, 'let's ride right foot forward through the waves.'"

"In surfing talk, *mondo* means big," I explained. "*Corduroy* is when the waves roll in, one right after the other. And *horizon* means high up."

"Oh. So you said, the waves are rolling in high," Cheryl said.

"Right! But enough surfing talk," I said. "It's time for some action! It's time for..."

"...surfing lessons!"

Ashley, Jenny, Nicole, and I learned how to ride the waves. Then we steered our boards onto shore. Cheryl was waiting on the beach, poking at the sand.

Jenny gaped at her in surprise. "Why didn't you surf?" she asked.

"I was checking out this sand," Cheryl said. "It's awesome! You can squish it in your toes or sift it through your fingers. And don't forget the most amazing thing you can do with it."

"What?" I asked.

"You can make great sand castles," Cheryl said. "Do you want to help me build one?"

"Yes!" we all shouted. We grabbed sand tools and started working on our sand castle.

Cheryl was right.

This *was* fun!

We scooped, dug, smoothed, and patted. In no time at all, we built a sand castle. And not just any sand castle.

We built the most stupendous, tremendous, incredible sand castle ever!

"We'd better have another swim to wash this sand off our hands," Jenny said.

"We can't do that," Cheryl replied. "We still haven't eaten—and I'm really hungry."

"Then we should have a luau," Nicole said.

"Do you mean it's time to say good-bye?" Jenny asked. She looked confused.

"You've got it wrong again!" Cheryl laughed. "Nicole didn't say *aloha*. She said a *luau*. I told you, a luau is a Hawaiian feast. Remember?"

"No, I forgot. So what? You don't have to be such a know-it-all!" Jenny exploded.

Cheryl looked shocked.

"Sorry, Cheryl," Jenny told her. "But sometimes you try to be an expert on *everything.*"

"And you keep telling us what to do," Nicole added. "It gets kind of annoying."

Cheryl burst into tears—and ran away!

We raced up the beach after her.

"Cheryl! Come back!" I yelled.

"Wait up!" Ashley called. "No one meant to hurt your feelings."

"Oh, yes, you did!" Cheryl stopped running. "I knew this would happen if we had a beach party!"

"What are you talking about?" I asked.

"I didn't want you to find out!" Cheryl said.

"Find out what?" I asked.

Cheryl took a deep breath. "I don't know how to swim!"

We all looked at Cheryl in surprise.

"You don't?" I asked.

"No," Cheryl told us. "That's why I kept telling you what to do. I was trying to find ways to get out of the water. I was afraid you wouldn't be friends with me if you found out."

Suddenly I started laughing.

So did Ashley.

Then Jenny and Nicole started laughing, too.

"What's so funny?" Cheryl asked.

"I can't believe you thought we wouldn't be friends with you!" I said.

"We don't care if you can't swim," Nicole said.

"Friends don't always have to like the same things," Jenny added.

"And friends who *can* swim can teach friends who *can't* swim," Ashley said.

"Everyone—back in the water for a swimming lesson!" I shouted.

We taught Cheryl everything we knew about swimming. Soon she was kicking her feet. She even put her head under the water to blow bubbles!

"I *love* swimming!" Cheryl exclaimed.

After swimming, Cheryl wanted to turn on some music and dance.

"Dance?" Jenny asked. "We can dance anytime. Let's do something we can only do in Hawaii."

"No problem," Nicole said. "In Hawaii, you can do a special dance where every move tells a story. I learned how to do it when I lived here. It's called the *hula*. Now, I'll show *you* how to do it!"

Nicole showed us the right way to move our arms and legs.

"What story does our hula tell?" I asked.

"This hula tells the story about us being friends," Nicole answered.

Yes!

"The hula is so much fun!" I said.

"I love dancing out a story," Ashley agreed.

"It *is* fun," Cheryl said. "But we have to stop now."

Ashley and I exchanged worried looks. Cheryl was the one who wanted to dance. Why was she trying to find something else to do *now?*

"Why should we stop?" I asked Cheryl.

"Because you told me to remind you when it was almost time to go," Cheryl said. "Remember?"

Oops!

"Thanks for reminding us," I said. "Because it's time to give everyone an amazing, beautiful surprise!"

"What could be more amazing than learning to swim in Waikiki?" Cheryl asked.

"Or more surprising than riding in a submarine?" Jenny added.

"Or more beautiful than dancing a hula about friendship?" Nicole said.

"These!" I replied. Ashley and I handed out our special party favors—silver necklaces with a pink dolphin charm. Everyone loved them!

"Three cheers for Mary-Kate and Ashley!" Jenny shouted.

"Thanks, guys," I said. "But this party isn't over yet."

"That's right," Ashley agreed. "We have one more surprise for you!"

"Another surprise? Wow!" Cheryl said.

Ashley handed everyone an incredible pink-and-purple flower lei!

"Lei rhymes with play," Ashley explained. "It's a special Hawaiian flower necklace."

Nicole sniffed at the flowers. *"Poo-ah!"* she said.

"Pooh-ah?" Cheryl frowned. "I think these flowers smell great."

Nicole laughed. *"Pua* is the Hawaiian word for flower," she explained.

"Oh! I didn't know that!" Cheryl's cheeks turned red. "I'm so embarrassed," she said.

"It's okay, Cheryl," I told her. "You don't have to know *everything."*

"Well, I *don't* know everything," Cheryl began. "But I do know this—Mary-Kate and Ashley throw the best parties anywhere!"

Now our beach party was really over. The blue water looked gold and red under the setting sun. It was time to gather our things together and head for home.

"Wait," Ashley said. She gazed across Waikiki. "How can we say good-bye to this beautiful beach?"

"We don't have to say good-bye," I told her. "We're bringing a little bit of Hawaii home with us. Something that no one can *ever* take away."

"Let me guess," Cheryl said. "Is it the spirit of aloha?"

"Yes! And this time, *aloha* means the spirit of friendship," Nicole added.

"Oh, everybody knows that!" I said.

Cheryl grinned. "Right," she said. "Because when it comes to friendship, we're *all* experts!"

We all giggled.

"You're right about that," Ashley said.

Then Ashley and I gave each of our friends a great big hug. We turned for one last look at Waikiki before we waved good-bye.

Aloha, Hawaii!

Hi—from both of us!

    Thanks for coming to our Hawaiian beach party. We hope that you'll wear your special dolphin necklace to remember the fun we all had—swimming, surfing, and dancing the hula.

    We can't wait to see you at our next fun party!

Love,

Mary-Kate and Ashley